This Walker book belongs to:

For dearest Maeve,
with all my love and thanks
on our wonderful journey
G. S.

For Aki and Satoru
D. McK.

First published 1978 by A & C Black Ltd

First published by Walker Books 2009
Walker Books Ltd, 87 Vauxhall Walk, London SE11 5HJ

This edition published 2010

1 2 3 4 5 6 7 8 9 10

Text © 1978 A & C Black Ltd and 2009 Gordon Snell
Illustrations © 1978 A & C Black Ltd and 2009 David McKee

The moral rights of the author and illustrator
have been asserted.

This book has been typeset in Avenir

Printed in China

British Library Cataloguing in Publication Data is available

ISBN 978-1-4063-1526-4

www.walker.co.uk

The King of Quizzical Island

Gordon Snell

illustrated by

David McKee

WALKER BOOKS
AND SUBSIDIARIES
LONDON • BOSTON • SYDNEY • AUCKLAND

The King of Quizzical Island
Had a most inquisitive mind.
He said, "If I sail to the edge of the world
I wonder what I'll find?"

He quizzed his wily old Wizard

And the Whispering Witches, too –

The Llama, the Leopard, the Lizard,

And the Owl – but none of them knew.

So the King of Quizzical Island

Made up his inquisitive mind

And he said, "I'll sail to the edge of the world

And find … what I shall find."

"I'll build myself a singular ship

   Made of wood from the Tea-Bag Tree,

   And I'll sail that ship to the edge of the world

   And see … what I shall see."

His fearful people pleaded.

They wept fat tears of woe.

Some said, "Remain!" and some, "Please stay!"

While others said, "Don't go!

"For it's quite well-known, and I've heard it said

By wise men, old and clever,

That those who sail to the edge of the world

Fall off – and fall for ever."

But the King of Quizzical Island

Said, "Tosh!" and "Bosh!" and "Twaddle!"

"For I can sail to the edge of the world

As sure as a duck can waddle."

So he built himself a singular ship

Made of wood from the Tea-Bag Tree –

And the rigging was a spider's web

And the rudder a bumble-bee.

The ship sailed out of the harbour

And the silken sails unfurled

As the King of Quizzical Island

Set sail for the edge of the world.

He sailed through waves as high as hills

For thirty days or more

Until at last, the ship was cast

On a higgledy-piggledy shore.

He found himself in a Jigsaw Land

Which lay there, all in pieces:

The blue bits might have been sea – or sky –

Or sheep, with ink-stained fleeces…

The green bits might have been grass – or leaves –

Or a snake, or a dragon's tail;

And the white bits might have been clouds – or snow –

Or the teeth of a smiling whale…

It took the King nine days and nights

To fit those bits in place –

Then he saw before him a river

And a smile lit up his face.

So he sailed up that Jigsaw River

And there, round the final bend,

He found himself in Vertical Land

Where everything stands on end.

The rivers go up like fountains

And the crocodiles stand on their tails

And the meadows tower like mountains

And the trains run on vertical rails.

The King said, "That's *one* way of using

Every inch of space you've got –

But it doesn't look very comfortable…"

And the crocodiles said, "It's not!"

So the singular ship sailed upwards

On a river tall and wide

And from the top of the river

It sailed down the other side.

It sailed through Hurricane Harriet

To the Sea of Dreadful Dreams,

Where the waves are for ever wailing,

And the Wild Wind sighs and screams,

Where the Sea-Horse turns into a Night-Mare

And prances upon the foam,

And gaggles of ghostly jelly-fish

Wobble their way back home.

"All things ghastly and ghoulish,"

Said the King, "I can put to flight —

They'll all feel extremely foolish

When I wake, and turn on the light."

He rang a hundred alarm-clocks,

And the Sky switched on the Sun,

And the Dreadful Dreams were ended

As quickly as they'd begun.

The wild wind sank to a whisper

And even the waves were shy

And the moon smiled down, benignly,

From the sleeping deeps of the sky.

The King of Quizzical Island

Sailed on, till he sighted land.

And the singular ship was beached upon

A handy, sandy strand.

He looked at the castle before him,

And knew he had seen it before –

And he said, "I've sailed to the edge of the world,

And arrived at my own back door!"

His people rushed out to greet him –

They gave him a rousing cheer:

And he said, "There *is* no edge of the world –

The world is a perfect sphere.

"I sailed out there in my singular ship,

And I'll tell you what I found.

I found I was back at my own back door –

So I've proved that the world is round!"

Everyone cheered and shouted,

They shouted and cheered and kissed.

Their King had come back from the edge of the world,

And proved it didn't exist!

Only the Owl was doubtful.

He said, "If the Earth is flat,

You *might* have sailed round in a circle,

And arrived where you started at."

The King of Quizzical Island

Was more than a bit put out.

He said, "Nonsense!" and "Bosh" and "Balderdash!"

But he still had a lingering doubt…

He said, "In Quizzical Island,

Answers must always be found –

And I have another perilous plan

To prove that the world is round."

"I shall build myself a singular spade,

Made of diamonds, ten feet wide,

And I'll dig a tunnel, far into the world,

And come out at the other side!"

The people, they gasped in wonder.

They said, "Gosh!" and "Gulp!" and "Glory!"

As the King began digging into the world...

But that is another story.

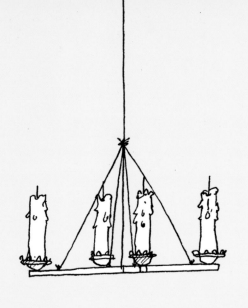

Gordon Snell

Gordon Snell has written lots of books for children and grown-ups, as well as songs, poems and plays. He also worked as a writer and interviewer for TV and radio. He says about *The King of Quizzical Island*, "Children are completely at home in the world of imagination and impossible situations. I hope they will enjoy the King's amazing adventures as much as I enjoyed creating them!" Gordon Snell lives in Dublin with his wife, the writer Maeve Binchey.

David McKee

David McKee started drawing cartoons for newspapers and magazines when he was still at art college. His first picture book, called *Two Can Toucan*, was published in 1964, and he went on to create some of the best-loved children's characters in the world, including Mr Benn, King Rollo and Elmer the Elephant. In 1980 he set up King Rollo Films, an award-winning animation studio. About *The King of Quizzical Island* he says, "I love the humour of this story and the way it provokes enquiry. All kings should be more like this one – asking questions then going out and seeking answers!" David McKee divides his time between England and France.